D0178411

04386320

A Cassava Republic Press edition 2016

First published in Belgium by De Eenhoorn
© Text and illustration: Mylo Freeman

Original Title: Prinses Arabella maakt kleuren
Copyright 2009 by Uitgeverij De Eenhoorn, Vlasstraat 17, B-8710 Wielsbeke (Belgium)

Translated from Dutch by Laura Watkinson

ISBN 978-1-911115-12-0

A CIP catalogue record for this book is available from the British Library.

The publisher gratefully acknowledges the support of the Dutch Foundation for Literature and the Mondriaan Fund.

N ederlands
letterenfonds
dutch foundation
for literature

All rights reserved. No part of this publication may be reproduced, stored in a retrieval system or transmitted in any form, or by any means, electrical, mechanical, photocopying, recording or otherwise without prior permission of the publishers.

www.cassavarepublic.biz

Mylo Freeman

Princess Arabella
Mixes Colours

The morning's first ray of sunshine slips into the room.

Princess Arabella stretches her arms and yawns.

She looks from the sun to the wall,
and from the wall to the floor.

From the floor to the mirror and
from the mirror to the dressing table.
From the dressing table to the chair and
from the chair to the bed.

"Yuk!" says Princess Arabella. "My bedroom looks
sooo boring!" She shakes her curly head. "I need to
do something about it!"

"Footmen, footmen, one, two, three! Come and do a job for me!"
The three footmen run to help the princess.
"I want lots and lots and LOTS of paint," says Princess Arabella,
waving her arms around. "Paint in every colour of the rainbow!"

The footmen bow deeply to Princess Arabella. Then, quick as a flash, they run to find some paint. They're back in an instant, carrying lots and lots of pots of paint. But Princess Arabella shakes her curly head. "Yuk, those aren't the colours I want!" She sticks her nose in the air.

"My dressing table needs to be pink.
But how can I make pink? Wait a
moment!

I know what to do! I'll mix some *red*,
and some *white* in this pot.
Stir it all up,
and look what I've got!"

The dressing table is *pink!*
As pink as raspberry ice cream.

Princess Arabella laughs and claps her hands.

"My mirror is going to be purple. That will look perfect. But how can I make purple? Wait a moment! I know what to do!

I'll mix some **red**, and some *blue* in this pot.

Stir it all up, and look what I've got!"

The mirror is **purple**! As bright and purple as a grape in the sun.

Princess Arabella is so happy. She jumps up and down. She wants to see every colour that there is, all of the colours in the world!

"I'll mix some *white*, and some *black* in this pot.
Stir it all up, and look what I've got!"

Elephant is grey! As *grey* as a stormy cloud.
Princess Arabella laughs.

The room already looks beautiful, so full of colour. She dances around.

"Now for my chair, that has to be orange. But how can I make orange? Wait a moment! I know what to do!

I'll mix some *yellow*, and some **red** in this
pot. Stir it all up...

... and look what I've got!"
The chair is *orange*!
As orange as a bowl of carrot soup.

"I have to do my bed too. And my bed's going to be green. But how can I make green?

Wait a moment! I know what to do!

I'll mix some *yellow*, and some *blue* in this pot.

Stir it all up, and look what I've got!"

Now the bed is *green*!

As green as tasty grass for a cow to munch on.

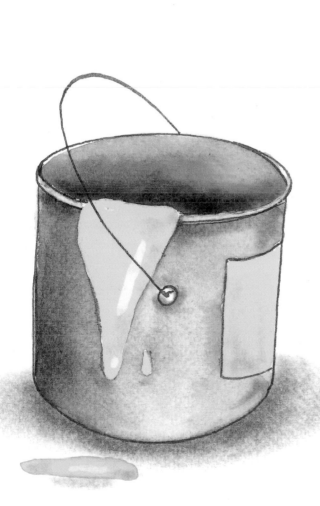
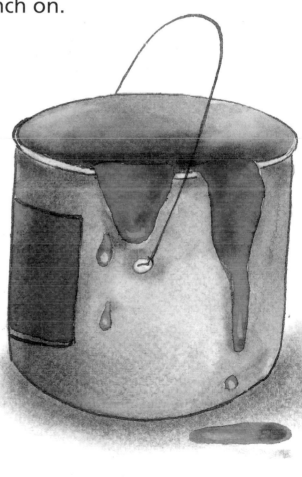

Everything looks wonderful, so fresh and so bright. But...
Oh dear... What's Princess Arabella doing now?! The pots, the
colours, the shiny paint, they're all flying through the air...
There are splatters and splashes everywhere! Princess Arabella feels
like crying...

"Arabella, sweetheart! Wake up!"
Huh? Who said that? Her mum, the Queen?

Princess Arabella stretches her arms and yawns.
She looks from the sun to the wall, and from the
wall to the floor.
From the floor to the mirror and from the mirror
to the dressing table. From the dressing table to
the chair and from the chair to the bed.

"Hmm, did I dream it all?" wonders Princess Arabella.

"But... Wow, my room looks sooo fabulous!"

Her bed is as green as tasty grass,
her chair as orange as carrot soup,
the mirror bright purple like a grape, the elephant as grey as a
cloud, and the dressing table as pink as raspberry ice cream…

"Didn't I really make any colours?

Was it all a dream?"

Princess Arabella shakes her curly head.

"So where did all those splatters and splashes come from...?"